Published by Willowisp Press, Inc.
401 E. Wilson Bridge Road, Worthington, Ohio 43085

Printed in the United States of America

10 9 8 7 6 5 4 3 2 1

ISBN 0-87406-227-6

Written and illustrated by the kindergarten class of Paul Mort Elementary School, Tampa, Florida: Vanessa Hannay, Darryl Johnson, Lynn Mangold, Lori Nelson, Kyle Paton, Stephanie Roblyer, Tara Schmidlen, Beth Sheubrooks, Benjamin Strowbridge, Paul Traci, Amanda Ward, Aaron Watkins.

Edited by Joanne M. McNeil, curriculum specialist in the Hillsborough County School District, Tampa, Florida. Paul Mort School is one of 94 elementary schools in the Hillsborough County School District. Paul Mort School strives to foster a love for reading and a continual growth in education.

This book is dedicated to all future kindergarten students who will attend Paul Mort School.

Once upon a time there was a boy named Fred. He was looking for a rainbow.

Fred looked and looked and looked. He could not find the rainbow.

Fred was sad. He asked his friend Jimmy to help him look for the rainbow.

Fred and Jimmy looked and looked for the rainbow. They could not find it.

Then one day it happened! It began to rain.

As the rain came down the sun came out!

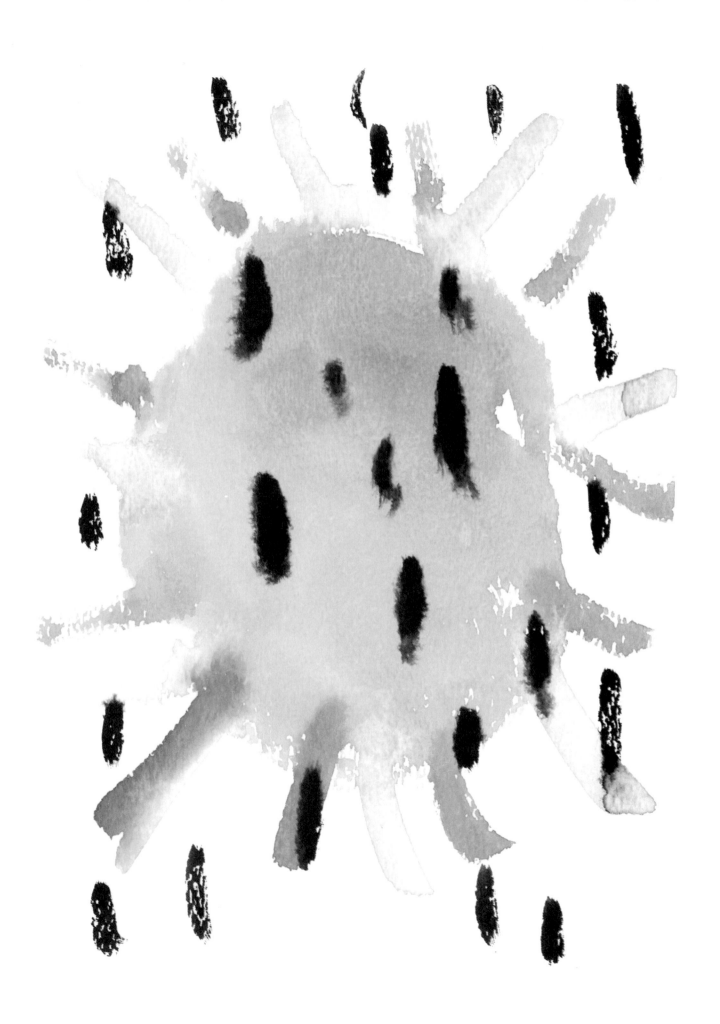

Before long a beautiful rainbow came out of the sky.

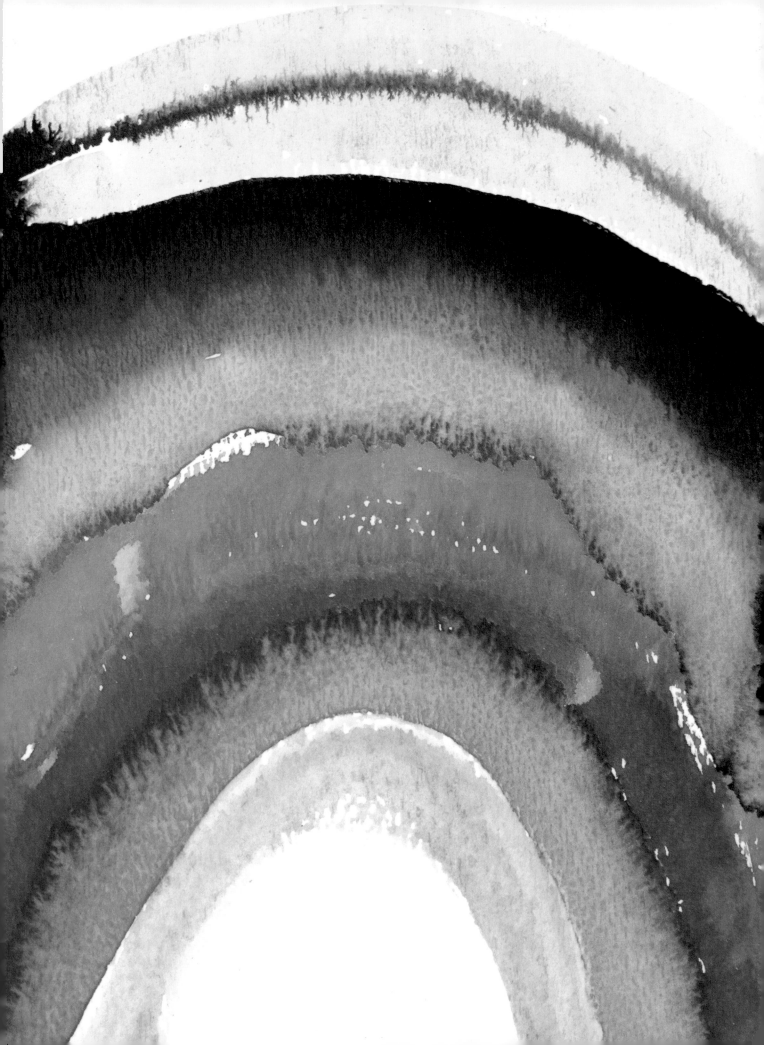

Fred and Jimmy were very happy. They found the rainbow!

Young Authors Week was established by SBF to recognize authors of children's books, especially children who write books. It is a time to focus on high-quality literature for young people and to encourage children to read and write.

To commemorate Young Authors Week, SBF sponsors a book writing competition in which groups of students submit original picture books for judging by a national panel of professionals in the field of children's literature.

For more information on Young Authors Week and the competition write to:

Young Authors Week
SBF, Inc.
401 E. Wilson Bridge Rd.
Worthington, Ohio 43085